Ypres, 1915

For Ben and Clare

M.M.

For my grandchildren

D.G.

First published 2014 in *The Great War: Stories Inspired by Objects from the First World War*
by Walker Books Ltd, 87 Vauxhall Walk, London SE11 5HJ

This illustrated edition published 2019

2 4 6 8 10 9 7 5 3 1

Text © 2014, 2018 Michael Morpurgo
Illustrations © 2018 David Gentleman

This book has been typeset in Sabon

Printed and bound in China

British Library Cataloguing in Publication Data:
a catalogue record for this book is available from the British Library

ISBN 978-1-4063-8314-0

www.walker.co.uk

MICHAEL MORPURGO

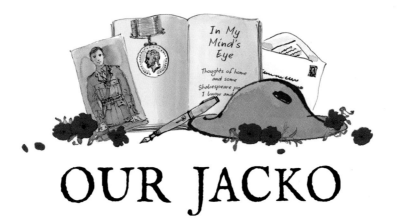

OUR JACKO

illustrated by David Gentleman

WALKER
BOOKS

I grew up with the tin hat. The first time I was aware of it, I was about three or four, and Otto, my big brother, was eight or nine, I suppose. Otto wore it almost constantly, not just when he was playing war games with his friends in the garden, but on his scooter, or cycling along, or sitting on the swing, even at meals sometimes – if he could get away with it. It hung by the strap on his special "Otto hook" by the back door, with his coat. It became "Otto's tin hat", and for a while it was his most treasured possession. He painted it bright red, the same red as the postman's van, and forbade me from wearing it or even touching it, threatening me with a Chinese burn, or death, if I did. I didn't want anything to do with it anyway. It was often the cause of quarrels between us, and we quarrelled a lot in those days. From the moment he told me, gleefully, that it was the helmet of a dead soldier, I hated the sight of it. There was a hole in it where he said a bullet had gone in and "done for him". I remember his very words, remember being horrified at the time and haunted by the thought of it. I still am.

Otto liked to annoy me, to provoke me, I think. He always knew that the sure way to get me riled was to say that war was exciting, that peace was boring. Often I'd lose my temper with him and it would end up as a shouting match – and once or twice, I'm ashamed to say, I'd find myself trying to punch him or kick him, which of course was just what he wanted.

He could taunt me then. I was a "hypocrite", or "a blood-thirsty little warmonger".

In time, thank goodness, Otto tired of his tin hat and his war games. My mother used it as a feeding bowl for the hens, but that didn't work because the hens could perch on the rim of it, and the corn would spill out onto the mud and too much of it was wasted. So then we used it for collecting the eggs instead. At least with the eggs in it, resting on a soft bed of hay, I couldn't see the hole. I hated that hole.

Then, for a while, my mother rigged it up outside the porch, as a hanging basket. The hole was perfect for that, she said, because the earth could drain well. It hung there by the front door for years. She grew white petunias in it that spilled over the side and cascaded down, like white tears. I would reach up and touch them for luck on my way out to school in the mornings. I liked that they were white. I liked white because it was the colour of peace. It seemed right and proper that the blood-red helmet, to me so much a symbol of the cruelty of war, was now being used as a flower basket, and could scarcely be seen through the abundance of white flowers; flowers of peace.

As we grew older, Otto and I continued to argue just as passionately about war and peace. There was less name calling, and I had learned by now that I had to keep my cool if I wanted to win an argument with him. He was a great reader of books, doing history A-level at school, and would blind me with his encyclopaedic knowledge of the past. He told me, rather patronizingly, that I would soon come to understand that although war might be unpleasant – even undesirable in some ways – it was sometimes necessary politically and justifiable morally. He said grandly that it was no good my being "a bleeding heart pacifist", that I would soon have to learn that the world was as it was, not how we would like it to be.

It was a relief to me when Otto went off to college, taking his burning ideas with him. He could stir them all up there, I thought, and leave me in peace at home.

Meanwhile, the tin hat, the original cause of all this sibling strife, had long since vanished. In its place my mother had a proper hanging basket, still growing petunias; still flowers of peace that brushed my face like a blessing as I walked in the front door. I liked that.

I was about fourteen when the tin hat reappeared. Had we not been moving house – from one side of Stratford to the other, not far – it is likely that the hat would never have been seen again. My mother discovered it at the bottom of a tea chest in the back of the garage, during the big sort-out as we were packing up to leave. Otto was not there to claim it, and I would cheerfully have chucked it in the skip along with everything else. It was Mr Macleod, our history teacher at school, who was, strangely, responsible for saving the tin hat from the skip, and for much of what happened next, too.

The day after my mother came across the tin hat in the tea chest, Mr Macleod announced a school history trip to the battlefields of the First World War in Belgium. It would be a three-day trip and was absolutely essential for our studies, he said. Secondly, because it was the centenary of the First World War he had decided to put on a full-scale school production of a  musical called *Oh, What a Lovely War!* He wanted as many of his history class as possible to be in it "whether you can act or not, whether you sing or not".

I went up to him after the lesson

and told him that I couldn't go to Belgium because it would be too expensive, and I couldn't be in his play because I didn't like acting. I didn't tell him the truth, which was that I had become committed to the idea of peace and simply hated the idea of visiting battlefields and the whole subject of war. Mr Macleod was quite dismissive and said I should think about it, that he'd speak to my mother about it.

When I got home that evening, Otto was back from college. He'd come home for the holidays, and there on the kitchen table beside the teapot was the tin hat.

"Mum said you wanted to chuck it," he said, stuffing himself with his favourite treacle cake. "That's my childhood, that tin hat. No one's chucking it."

Here we go again, I thought. "Best thing to do with it," I told him. "It belongs in the skip, like war does."

"Very profound," Otto mumbled, his mouth full.

And then I told them all about Mr Macleod's plans for the school trip and the play.

"'S'all history is, one long, lousy war," I said. "I'm not going to Belgium, anyway."

That was when war almost broke out in the family and the two of them ganged up against me.

"You should go," my mother said, "I think everyone should go at least once in their lifetime. It's part of our history, part of who we are. That war changed the world."

"Surely," Otto joined in, "if you want what you say you want – a world at peace – you have to understand the consequences of a world at war. Plenty of consequences buried out there in the battlefields of the First World War – millions of them. Just because you don't approve of it, that's no reason not to face it, however sad it makes you feel, however angry."

I didn't agree with Otto but I listened to him. He wasn't teasing me or patronizing me. I felt he was at least taking me more seriously.

I think it was partly because of what Otto said to me, and how he said it, that I changed my mind about the school trip: the next day I put my name down for it. But there was another reason, too, even more compelling: the strange and timely reappearance of the tin hat, Otto's old war helmet. It was still there on the kitchen table the next morning at breakfast before I went off to school. Otto wasn't up, no one was. I sat there eating my muesli and staring at the hole in the helmet. This helmet had belonged to a soldier in the First World War – a soldier who had died, a soldier only a little older than me, some mother's son, some child's father. He would be out there somewhere, buried on the battlefield. I would go.

That morning, Mr Macleod asked us to do some research when we got home. "Go online," he said. "Have a look at your family tree. Dig about a bit. Ask your mum and dad, grandparents, aunties, uncles. Do you have a relation, a great-great-grandfather, who was a soldier or a sailor, or in the Royal Flying Corps, maybe? Did they die in the war somehow, or did they come home? Do you have a great-great-grandmother who was a nurse at the front or who worked in a munitions factory? I want to set up an exhibition in the library. 'The War to End all Wars', we'll call it. Bring in anything you can find. Old photos, medals, badges, letters. We want to look into the faces of those who lived then, read their words, hear their voices, as far as we can. We want to know how it was to be them, to live through those times. They were there. They can tell us."

I had never known Mr Macleod to be so passionate, so

inspiring. He was, I had always thought, a bit of a dry old stick. I could see – we all could – that this wasn't simply dusty old history for him. He wanted each of us to go with him on a voyage of discovery into the past so that, as he put it, "we can better understand our present and make a better future. It's what those millions of 'the mouthless dead' would have wanted."

When I got home that evening and told everyone about the exhibition, I was amazed at Otto's response. I'd never seen him like this, so keen and helpful. He said at once that our tin hat had to be "the star of the show". He wasted no time and set about removing the red paint so that it wouldn't look like a kid's toy any more. He said it should be khaki again, its proper colour, its original colour. It didn't take him long. The toxic odour of paint stripper filled the house all evening.

But my mother wasn't at all sure about it. "We don't really know it's a helmet from the First World War," she said. "It could be from the Second World War – they looked just about the same, didn't they?"

At that, my father turned the television off and sat up, suddenly taking notice. "No, no," he said. "It's definitely First World War. Belonged to Grandpa Tom's grandfather. Jacko. We always called him 'Our Jacko' in the family when I was growing up. That's what I was always told when I was little: that Our Jacko didn't come home but his helmet did. Brought home by his best friend. That's how come we got it."

"But that could just be a story, couldn't it?" my mother said.

"No, no. There's a photo of Our Jacko somewhere," my father replied, getting up. "I remember it. And some other stuff Grandpa Tom left us. Haven't seen hide nor hair of it for years. There were a couple of medals, too, if I remember right, and a book, a little notebook full of writings you couldn't hardly read, so I never did. And yes, there was a shell case, made of brass or metal or something. Mum used to polish it up and put flowers in it. She always called it Our Jacko's vase. But it wasn't a vase, not really. Grandpa Tom always told me it was a shell case that belonged to Our Jacko, and that it came back with his helmet and things."

"What happened to it?" my mother asked.

"Well," said my father, "so far as I know, it was all in an old leather suitcase. We had it up in the attic once, I know we did."

My mother looked suddenly aghast. "I threw it in the skip this morning," she said. "Thought it was empty."

We retrieved the suitcase at once and opened it up on the kitchen table. It smelled of mould and decay. At first it looked as if it was full of nothing but old Christmas decorations – paper stars, a plastic angel, a Father Christmas without a head, some glitter balls and a wooden crib – but underneath all these long-forgotten remnants of Christmases past lay what looked like a large metal vase.

"See?" said my father. "That's it, that's the shell case." He held it up.

Otto took it from him. "Look, Dad, it's got an engraving on it, and writing, too! Can't hardly read it. Too grimy. It looks like a shell case all right. Must be. And Grandma used it for flowers! Weird or what?"

"No, it's not weird," I said. "That's the best thing it could be used for. She was turning a weapon of war into a flower vase."

But they weren't listening to me. Hidden away under more Christmas decorations, my mother had found a large brown envelope. She gave it to my father. He opened it and took something out.

"It's here," he said. "The notebook." He turned to the first page and read out loud: "*This book belongs to Lt Jack Morris, actor, Shakespeare Memorial Theatre, Stratford-upon-Avon.* That's Our Jacko! It's got a title: *In my mind's eye. Thoughts of home and some Shakespeare poems I know and love.*" He turned the notebook over and looked at the back. "It says, *To whoever may find this, please return it to the theatre in Stratford, where I work; or to Ellie, my dear wife, and to Tom, our little son, at Mead Cottage, Charlecote Road, Hampton Lucy. I should be for ever grateful. Jack Morris, Lt Sherwood Foresters. Ypres. Belgium.* It's his writing, Our Jacko's handwriting, from a hundred years ago," my father said, in a whisper almost.

At that moment, something fell out of the notebook onto the table. I picked it up. It was a photograph. A young man

In My
Mind's
Eye

Thoughts of home
and some
Shakespeare poems
I know and love.

in uniform stood there, hand resting on a table beside him, stiff and stern, looking at me out of his black-and-white world. Looking me straight in the eye, knowing – I could see it – that he was going to die, that he was telling me so, too. He looked more like a boy dressing up than a soldier.

"Here," my father went on, handing the notebook to Otto, "you read it. It's in pencil. I can't read it too well."

Otto began to read in a hushed voice. We all listened.

"18 June 1915

Dearest Ellie,

I hope one day, when all this is over, to come home and bring this little notebook with me. Should it come home without me, then you will know for ever how much you and little Tom are in my thoughts; you, and the walks we went on down the river, and the poems we loved to read together. I am determined to write nothing of this place or of the war. It is a nightmare that one day I shall wake from and then forget. And if I don't wake, then you shall never know. I don't want you ever to know.

I want mostly to write of the good times, to see them and you again in my mind's eye; to read them again and again, to remind me that there is goodness and beauty and love in this world, to remind me of you and of our Tom."

Otto paused for a moment, and then read on.

"Our first walk together:

In my mind's eye... I am walking down through the meadows along the river beyond Half Moon Spinney, where I walked when I was a boy, where I walked with you, Ellie, where one day you and Tom and I will all walk together; and I will pick a buttercup and hold it under his chin to see if he likes butter, or pick a dandelion clock and puff on it to tell the time.

It is best as it is now, in the early morning, the cows wandering legless through the mist. I am alone with them and with birdsong. I am walking where Will Shakespeare walked, where he fished, where he dreamed the dreams of his plays and his poems, along the bank where he sat and wrote, maybe. A kingfisher flew for him too, and it flew for us once, do

you remember, Ellie? As it flies for me now, in my mind's eye. Straight like an arrow on fire out of the mist. And a heron lifts off unhurried. Heron, kingfisher, they were both taught to fish as I was, by their fathers – and mothers; and I shall teach Tom, when I come home. The river flows slow now, in gentle eddies, unhurried. She's taking her time. The aspen trees are quivering in the breeze. The whole world along the river trembles with life."

No one spoke, not for a long time. Otto was turning the pages of the notebook.

"There's lots of them, lots of walks along the river, all in his mind's eye," he said. "That's how he begins each walk: 'In my mind's eye'. That's Shakespeare, isn't it? I did it at school. It's from *Hamlet*, I think. And then there's poems, lots of them. I think they're Shakespeare too. He must have learned them as an actor. He's written them all down. Listen:

"Over hill, over dale,
Through bush, through briar,
Over park, over pale,
Through flood, through fire.
I do wander everywhere
Swifter than the moon's sphere…"

"We've been to the theatre in Stratford, haven't we?" said my mother. "We've been where he acted. Can I see?" She took the book from Otto and looked through it. "All the poems he loved most, and all the walks he loved, and the people he loved," she said. "And all in this little book. All the good in his life in this book. He knew the river like the back of his hand," she added.

"All the flowers and all the birds. All the places we know, too. He was there! Listen to this.

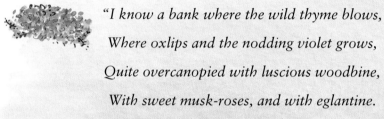

"I know a bank where the wild thyme blows,
Where oxlips and the nodding violet grows,
Quite overcanopied with luscious woodbine,
With sweet musk-roses, and with eglantine.
There sleeps Titania sometime of the night,
Lulled in these flowers with dances and delight;
And there the snake throws her enamelled skin,
Weed wide enough to wrap a fairy in;
And with the juice of this I'll streak her eyes,
And make her full of hateful fantasies."

"That's from *A Midsummer Night's Dream*, I think," she added.

"I acted in that once myself," my father mumbled, "at school. I was Bottom, with a donkey's head and donkey ears."

"Perfect casting then, Dad," Otto said, and we laughed at that. It was a relief for all of us to be able to laugh.

From each excerpt she read out we learned a little more about Our Jacko. He had done a lot of falling in love, we discovered: with Shakespeare first, after he saw a play in the theatre at Stratford when he was twelve – *Henry V*, it was – and then with acting from that day on; with walking; with boating; and later, when he was older, with Ellie, who worked with costumes at the theatre. He'd met her when he first acted in walk-on parts on the stage at Stratford, as a spear carrier, or a courtier, or a soldier.

I had been looking at the photo of Our Jacko all the time my mother was reading. It was as if I could hear his voice in every word. I turned the photo over. On the back was written: *Jack Morris, my husband, father of Tom, son, actor, soldier. Our Jacko. Born: 23 September 1892, Stratford. Killed: 20 October 1915, Ypres. He may have no known grave, but he rests in our hearts for ever.*

We then had the most intense family discussion I can ever remember, about what I should or should not take into school for the exhibition. My father said I could take in the tin hat and the shell case but that the rest was private and too precious. I argued that no one had thought the notebook precious when it had been stuffed away in an old envelope for years.

It surprised me how adamant my father was about it – but I was even more surprised when Otto piped up in my defence.

"The photo and the notebook may be precious and unique and irreplaceable," he said, "but they tell Our Jacko's story. Everyone should know his story."

And he came up with a solution. We would photocopy the photo and all the pages of the notebook.

The tin hat was already khaki again, hardly a fleck of red

paint to be seen thanks to the paint-stripping job Otto had done. Now he took on the cleaning of the shell case. Within an hour or so, the tarnish of a century was rubbed and polished away. It shone now; it gleamed. The engraving turned out to be of flowers all around – poppies, they looked like – and above them was a name: YPRES. The place where

Our Jacko had been killed, the place where I was going on my school trip to the battlefields.

At the bottom of the shell case, the writing, now quite legible, told us more about when and where it was made: 1915. PATRONEFABRIK. KARLSRUHE. My father thought Karlsruhe must be the name of a German town. We googled it to be sure. He was right.

"Same year, isn't it?" said Otto. "The year Our Jacko was killed. This was a German shell, fired in Ypres."

No one said anything. My mother was turning the pages of the notebook.

"He's written this poem out more than once," she said. "Hardly surprising. I mean, being out there, in that war, in those trenches, never knowing if this was your last day. From *Cymbeline*, I think." Then she read it.

"Fear no more the heat o' th' sun,

Nor the furious winter's rages.

Thou thy worldly task hast done,

Home art gone, and ta'en thy wages.

Golden lads and girls all must,

As chimney-sweepers, come to dust.

Fear no more the frown o' th' great,

Thou art past the tyrant's stroke.

Care no more to clothe and eat,

To thee the reed is as the oak.

The sceptre, learning, physic, must

All follow this and come to dust.

Fear no more the lightning flash,

Nor th' all-dreaded thunder-stone.

Fear not slander, censure rash.

Thou hast finished joy and moan.

All lovers young, all lovers must

Consign to thee and come to dust.

No exorcisor harm thee,

Nor no witchcraft charm thee.

Ghost unlaid forbear thee.

Nothing ill come near thee.

Quiet consummation have,

And renownèd be thy grave."

Later that evening I was alone with my mother in the kitchen. There was a song playing on a CD, one of her favourites. It was one I was fed up with hearing – I knew it too well. She was singing along.

"All around my hat I will wear the green willow, and all around my hat..."

As she was jigging about to the rhythm, I happened to look out of the window at the window box where she grew her tulips, always white – she loved white tulips. Somehow the words of that song and the white of the tulips wove themselves into an idea that fast became a plan, and one I was very soon determined to carry out. But it wasn't just the tulips and the song that made up my mind; it was the thought of Our Jacko dying so young, only twenty-three; Our Jacko, who had walked the banks of the river where I walked, acted in the theatre I had been to; who never came home, who had no known grave, who never walked the riverbank again with Ellie or Tom.

There was one poem in particular that I read over and over again. It wasn't about the countryside along the river, like so many of the others, but rather about the night before a battle. So he had written about the war, despite his resolve not to. I imagined him reading it to himself by candlelight in his dugout the night before he died. He had written in the margin, *Henry V. I was a soldier in this play. And now I play a soldier.*

From camp to camp through the foul womb of night
The hum of either army stilly sounds,
That the fixed sentinels almost receive
The secret whispers of each other's watch.
Fire answers fire, and through their paly flames
Each battle sees the other's umbered face.
Steed threatens steed, in high and boastful neighs
Piercing the night's dull ear, and from the tents
The armourers, accomplishing the knights,
With busy hammers closing rivets up,
Give dreadful note of preparation.
The country cocks do crow, the clocks do toll
And the third hour of drowsy morning name.

I took the notebook up to bed with me that night and read it from cover to cover, following in my mind's eye where he had walked, seeing his face in my head with every word. Every walk he wrote about, every poem he wrote down, made me more certain I was doing the right thing.

I was up early before the others. After quite a search, I found the ribbon I was looking for in a drawer in the kitchen and I took the tulips I needed from the window box. By the time I got to school, the trestle tables for the exhibition were up in the library, covered in Union Jacks from end to end. Mr Macleod was busying himself making a comprehensive list of all the exhibits. There were medals – lots of those; buttons and badges; one or two

sepia photographs; something that looked like a garden hoe but that he said was a trenching tool; and a large photo Mr Macleod had discovered himself, he told me, of children from our school photographed in front of the old block. Some of the boys were in sailor's uniform and the girls were in smock dresses; all hollow-cheeked and unsmiling, all wearing great hobnail boots.

"That was taken in 1914," he told me. "Twenty-three of them went. Eight never came back. Him … him … him. And her, too … she was killed in a Zeppelin raid on London, where she had gone to live with her auntie. What've you brought in, then?"

But before I could tell him, he was distracted by the headteacher.

It didn't take me long to put out our family exhibits. I found some water for the shell case and arranged the tulips. I tied the white ribbon around the tin hat, leaned the photo of Our Jacko up against the shell case and placed the notebook beside it. Then I wrote on the labels Mr Macleod had provided:

Lt Jack Morris. Sherwood Foresters. Son, husband, father, actor at Stratford, soldier. Killed 1915, Ypres.

Beside the tin hat I propped up the card on which I had written out the poem the evening before, in bed:

All around his hat
I will wear the white ribbon,
All around his hat
For a twelve month and a day.
And if anyone should ask me
The reason why I'm wearing it,
It's all for Our Jacko
Who's far, far away.

We went to Ypres a few weeks later and saw the museum there – In Flanders Fields, it's called. I'd never cried in a museum before. We stood in windswept war cemeteries, walked along the lines of gravestones, read the names, saw how young they were, how many there were. Thousand upon thousand. Mr Macleod took us to the place where the Christmas truce of 1914 had taken place, where both sides had met in the middle and exchanged gifts, played a game of football and sung carols. He showed us where the trenches must have once been, the wire, the shell holes. We were standing in no-man's-land, he said.

He read us a poem by Carol Ann Duffy about the Christmas truce, and we listened in silence because it was so powerful, and because every one of us knew from the break in his voice that Mr Macleod loved the poem.

When he finished, he said, "They said this was to be the war to end all wars. I'm thinking that all the fellows lying here, on both sides, hoped and believed it was true. But it wasn't. We don't learn."

I think it was listening to that poem about the Christmas truce out there in that field that changed my mind, maybe; that and knowing – as I did now – all about my great-great grandfather, about Our Jacko. I decided there and then that I wanted to be in the play after all.

On our last evening we went to hear the bugles played under the Menin Gate, where they play them every evening. We stood there with hundreds of others, the bugles echoing under the great arch, and as they played I looked upwards to where the sound was rising. And as I looked, I read the names, each one – like Our Jacko – a son, a husband maybe, a father maybe. I saw his name without even looking for it, as if he

was showing me. JACK MORRIS, LT. He was there in among all the other thousands of those who had no known grave.

As the last echoes of the bugles died away, I knew what I had to do, what I felt Our Jacko was telling me to do.

I got home. I talked to Otto about it, asked what he thought – and I'm glad I did, because he came with me the next day, the tin hat in his rucksack, as we followed in Our Jacko's footsteps all the way from Hampton Lucy to Stratford along the river, so far as we could. We stopped from time to time as he had done, maybe where he had, and read to one another from his notebook. And we ended our journey in a rowing boat, as we knew he and Ellie had done so often together, and then walked through the gaggle of ducks and geese, up the steps into the theatre.

Otto said I should do the talking because it had been my idea. The problem was finding the right person to talk to.

I think we must have looked rather bewildered and lost, because in the end, as luck would have it, the right person found us. She was, she told us, the "front-of-house manager". I had no idea what that meant but it sounded important, so I told her why we had come.

"Well, you see," I began, "our great-great-grandfather, Our Jacko – Jack Morris, really – was an actor here in 1914 and he was killed in the war, and our great-great-grandmother worked here too, in the theatre. She did the costumes, and that's how they met. And we saw *Henry V* here once, like Our Jacko did, and the soldiers wore hats in it, tin hats like this one."

I took the tin hat out of the rucksack and showed it to her. "This is Our Jacko's helmet from the First World War, and I thought – we thought, Otto and me – that it belonged here, so maybe one day it can be used in a play. Because Our

Jacko loved acting, loved Shakespeare, loved the theatre."

I held it out to her and she took it, and for many moments she stood there, looking down at it and saying nothing.

Then she said, "I wonder, could you wait a moment?"

So we did. We waited for quite some time before she came back and asked us to follow her. She led us through the doors into the theatre itself. The stage was empty of scenery but it was lit up, and on the stage were dozens of actors, all looking at us as we walked towards them. A couple of them helped us up onto the stage.

"Tell them what you told me," said the front-of-house manager. "The whole story."

So, with a little encouragement from Otto, I did.

I finished by reading the last poem in Our Jacko's notebook, from *Love's Labour's Lost*. The last one he ever wrote down. There were a few scribbled words above it.

I read those, too.

"It is cold this morning, and bright, snow carpeting the
mud. No guns. The world is almost beautiful again.

When icicles hang by the wall,
And Dick the shepherd blows his nail,
And Tom bears logs into the hall,
And milk comes frozen home in pail;
When blood is nipped, and ways be foul,
Then nightly sings the staring owl:
Tu-whit, tu-woo! – a merry note,
While greasy Joan doth keel the pot.

When all aloud the wind doth blow,
And coughing drowns the parson's saw,

And birds sit brooding in the snow,
And Marian's nose looks red and raw;
When roasted crabs hiss in the bowl,
Then nightly sings the staring owl:
Tu-whit, tu-woo! – a merry note,
While greasy Joan doth keel the pot."

When I had finished, one of the actors started to clap, then another, then all of them. And we knew they were clapping for Our Jacko and for Ellie, so Otto and I clapped too.

We went home on the bus, silent in our thoughts, with two free tickets to *A Midsummer Night's Dream*. Otto looked over and smiled at me. I smiled back. We were happy.

Michael Morpurgo OBE was 2003–2005 Children's Laureate, has written over 100 books and is the winner of many awards, including the Whitbread Children's Book Award, the Smarties Book Prize, the Blue Peter Award and the Red House Children's Book Award. His books are translated and read around the world and his hugely popular novel *War Horse* is now both a critically acclaimed stage play and a highly successful film. Michael and his wife, Clare, live in Devon.

David Gentleman is an artist, illustrator, designer and author. His books include *David Gentleman's Britain* and related books on London, the British coastline, Paris, India and Italy. He is also known for his wood engraved platform-length mural at Charing Cross, one of London's most striking underground station designs, and he has designed British postage stamps and coins. David's work is represented in Tate Britain, the British Museum and the Victoria and Albert Museum among many others. He lives in London.

Ypres, 2015